So many dynamos (sō men´ē dī´nuh-mōz´), *1. a phrase which reads the same backward and forward, i.e., a palindrome. 2. a whole slew of electric generators.*

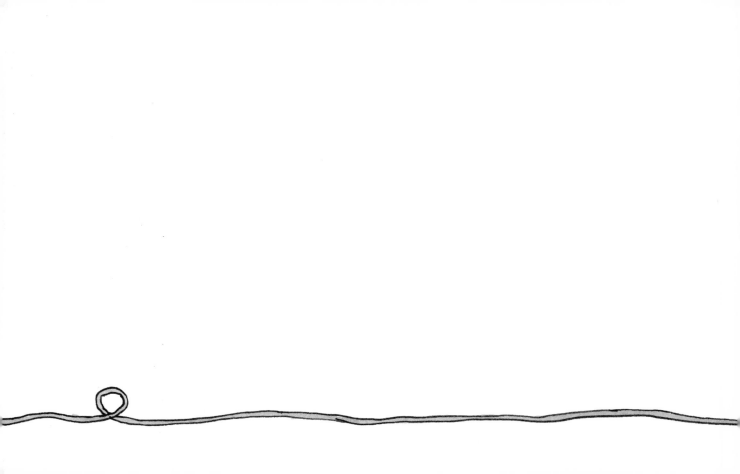

SO MANY DYNAMOS!

SO

MANY DYNAMOS!

and Other Palindromes
by JON AGEE

A Sunburst Book

Farrar · Straus · Giroux

To Dan Feigelson

PORCH CROP

NATE BIT
A TIBETAN

STIFF FITS

A SANTA AT NASA

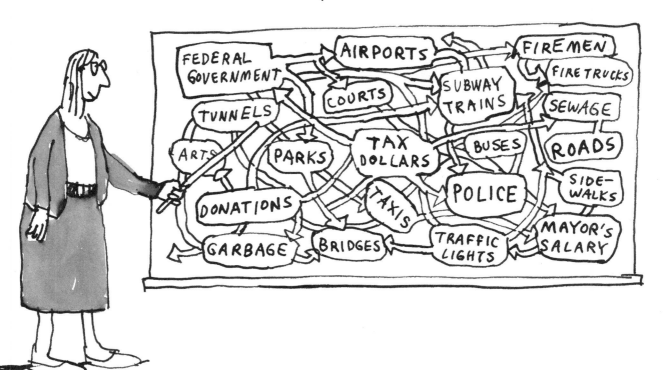

OTTO MADE
NED A MOTTO

DALI
LAD

RATS PARADED
A RAP STAR

STRAW
WARTS

AMORAL
AROMA

REMARKABLE MELBA KRAMER

TIN SANITARY RAT, IN A SNIT

TOO FAR
AFOOT

TRAIL
GUIDE
includes
fold-out
map,
compass,
dry socks

TEN ALPS
BORDERED
ROB'S PLANET

DAD'S DAD'S
DAD

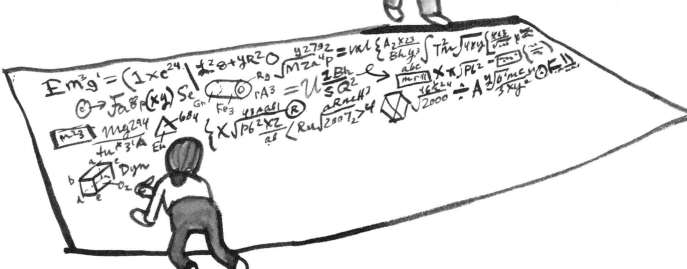

TOO HOT
TO HOOT

EMU FUME

"NO"S IN
UNISON

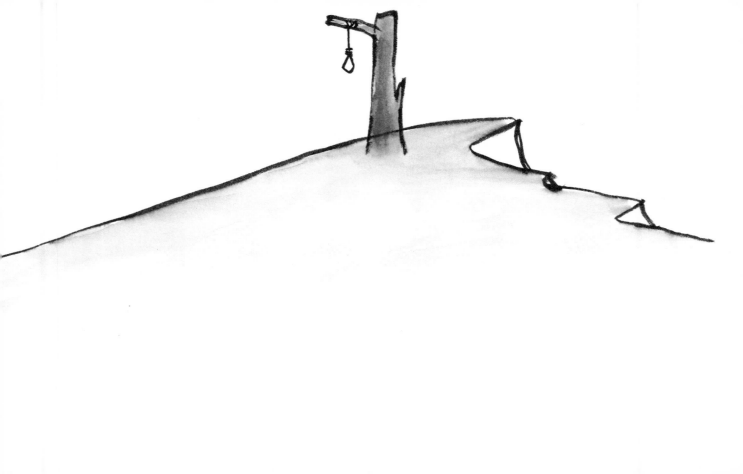

Thanks to
Tom Bassmann, John Baumann, Dan Covino,
Mel Hess, Yishane Lee, J. A. Lindon, and Gilly Youner
for their palindromes, and to Henry Finkelstein and
Melissa Mead for their contributions.

With apologies to Boston Red Sox fans

LEVI'S is a registered trademark of Levi Strauss & Co.